A Pattern for Pepper

Julie Kraulis

TUNDRA BOOKS

Tundra Books, a division of Random House of Canada Limited, a Penguin Random House Company

Library and Archives Canada Cataloguing in Publication

Kraulis, Julie, author, illustrator

A pattern for Pepper / Julie Kraulis.

Issued in print and electronic formats.

ISBN 978-1-101-91756-5 (hardback).—ISBN 978-1-101-91758-9 (epub)

I. Title.

PS8621.R37P38 2017   jc813'.6   C2016-905236-2

C2016-905237-0

Published simultaneously in the United States of America by Tundra Books of Northern New York, a division of Random House of Canada Limited, a Penguin Random House Company

Library of Congress Control Number 2016948351

Edited by Samantha Swenson
The artwork in this book was rendered in oils and graphite on board.
The text was set in Adobe Caslon.

Printed and bound in China

www.penguinrandomhouse.ca

1   2   3   4   5   21   20   19   18   17

SOURCES

Susan Meller and Joost Elffers, *Textile Designs: Two Hundred Years of European and American Patterns Organized by Motif, Style, Color, Layout, and Period* (Harry N. Abrams, 2002).

Lesley Jackson, *20th Century Pattern Design, 2nd Edition* (Princeton Architectural Press, 2011).

Janet Wilson, *Classic and Modern Fabrics: The Complete Illustrated Sourcebook* (Thames and Hudson, 2010).

Penguin
Random
House
TUNDRA BOOKS

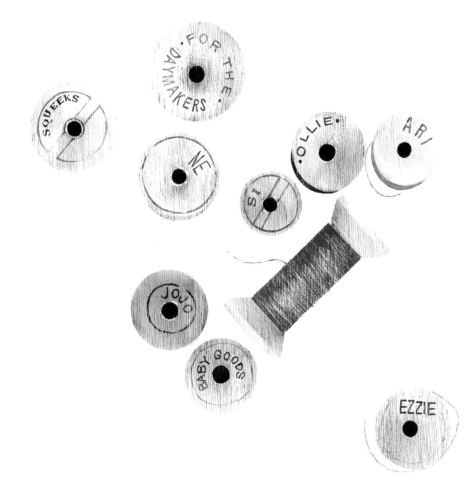

Pepper needs a dress for a very special occasion. Only the most perfect dress will do! So she and her mother have come to Mr. Taylor's shop to have one made just for her.

It's Pepper's first time at Mr. Taylor's, her family's favorite tailor shop and the oldest and busiest in town. A bell tinkles as Pepper and her mother step into the warm and cozy store.

"Hello. I'm Pepper, and I need a dress for a very special occasion," she says.

"I'm pleased to meet you, Pepper," says Mr. Taylor. "You've come to the right place!"

"First things first: let's take your measurements," Mr. Taylor says.

Pepper stands on the stool while Mr. Taylor starts measuring.

"Next we'll need to choose the fabric for your dress. Fabrics are textiles, and textiles come in all sorts of patterns," he says. "Let me show you what I've got!"

"Patterns are everywhere!" says Mr. Taylor. "See the floor? It's a herringbone pattern, inspired by the skeleton of a herring fish. We could use a herringbone fabric for your dress. What do you think?"

"Fish are nice, but it's too cold underwater f

No thank you," says Pepper.

How about seersucker, like your mom's dress? It's perfect for this warm summer weather," Mr. Taylor says, opening the window. "The word seersucker comes from the Persian *shir o shakkar*, which means 'milk and sugar,' because of its smooth and bumpy textures."

I like my tea strong, without milk and sugar. No thank you," says Pepper.

"What pattern is your suit?"
Pepper asks.

"Ah! This is tartan. It comes from
Scotland and is woven with wool
in checked patterns. Tartan is
used for clothing, hats and even
bagpipes."

"Oh, no. Bagpipes are just
TOO LOUD! No thank you,"
says Pepper.

"The rug you're lying on is a houndstooth pattern," says Mr. Taylor. "It has small, four-pointed checks that make shapes like hounds' teeth. My grandfather wore this fabric while hunting in the Scottish Lowlands. Would houndstooth work for you?"

"I like dogs. But special occasions require more color, I think. No thank you," says Pepper.

"Who is this?" asks Pepper.

"Meet Ikat," says Mr. Taylor. "He's named after a fabric with a fancy hand-dying process. *Ikat* means 'to bind, to knot, to wind around' in the Malay-Indonesian language."

"That sounds complicated! Yesterday my hair was so knotty it took four hours to sort it all out. No thank you," says Pepper.

"What pattern are my socks?" Pepper asks with her feet in the air.

"Your sock pattern goes back to the seventeenth century or earlier in the western Scottish Highlands. Argyle is a design of overlapping diamonds and diagonal lines, and it's often used for golf clothes."

"I do like to play golf. But I think I want my dress pattern to be prettier than that. No thank you," says Pepper.

"See that man walking by outside?" says Mr. Taylor. "His suit is a pinstripe pattern. Some baseball teams use pinstripes too—like the White Sox. How would you like pinstripe for your dress?"

"He looks kind of glum. I need something extra fun for my special day! No thank you," says Pepper.

"Take a look at this photo of your grandma," Mr. Taylor says. "She married a fellow from Switzerland, and I made her wedding dress from a textile created there called dotted swiss. It's a delicate, lightweight fabric with a small dotted pattern woven on top."

"Ooh, pretty! But too plain for me.
No thank you," says Pepper.

"The chair you're sitting on is made with toile, a fabric from France with hand-drawn scenes of the French countryside," says Mr. Taylor.

"Hmm. This countryside looks too busy. No thank you," says Pepper. "Mr. Taylor, what if I don't like ANY of these patterns?"

"Not to worry, Pepper," Mr. Taylor says. "Your perfect pattern is in here somewhere! So let's see . . . your pattern has to be pretty and strong. It has to be warm and fun. Not too plain, but not too complicated either. Colorful but not too busy . . . hmm." He stops and thinks.

"Aha! I have just the thing!" He pulls a bolt of fabric from the shelf.

Pepper's eyes light up. "That's it!" she says. "That's the one!"

Pepper and Mr. Taylor get to work
sketching designs for the dress.

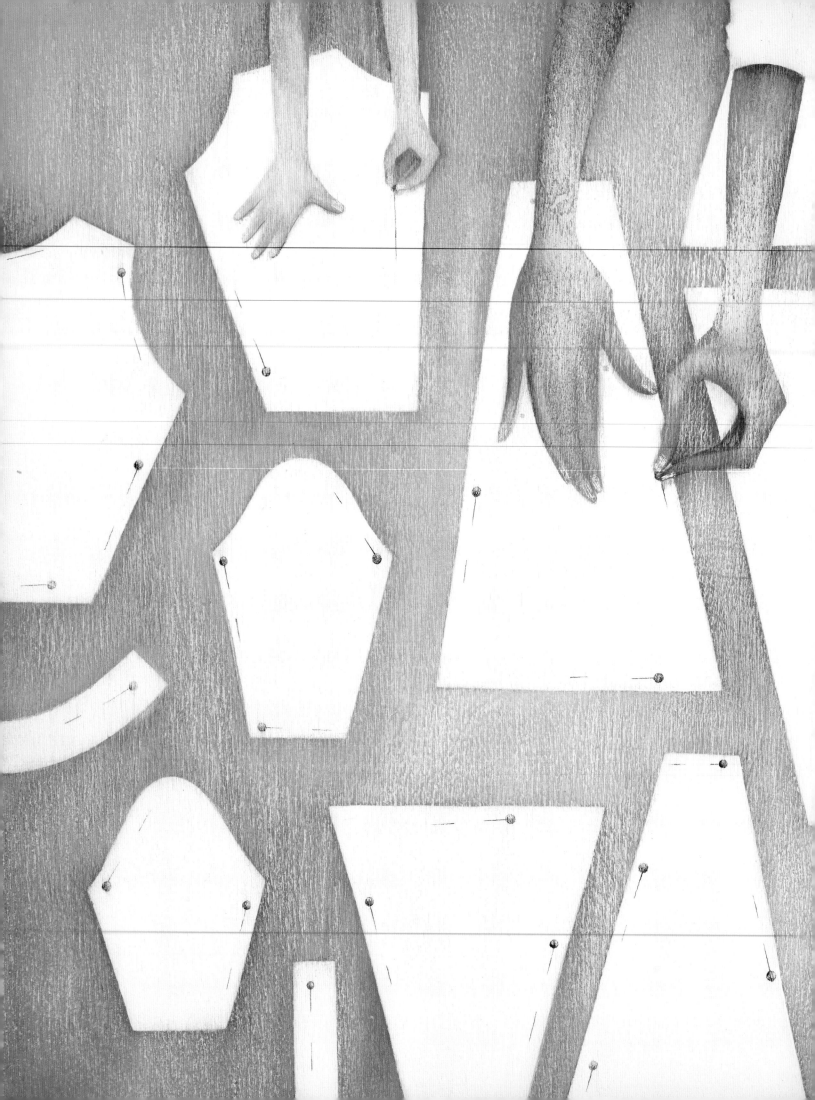

When they've finished their design, Mr. Taylor draws it on a huge roll of paper. He cuts out the pieces and pins them to the fabric.

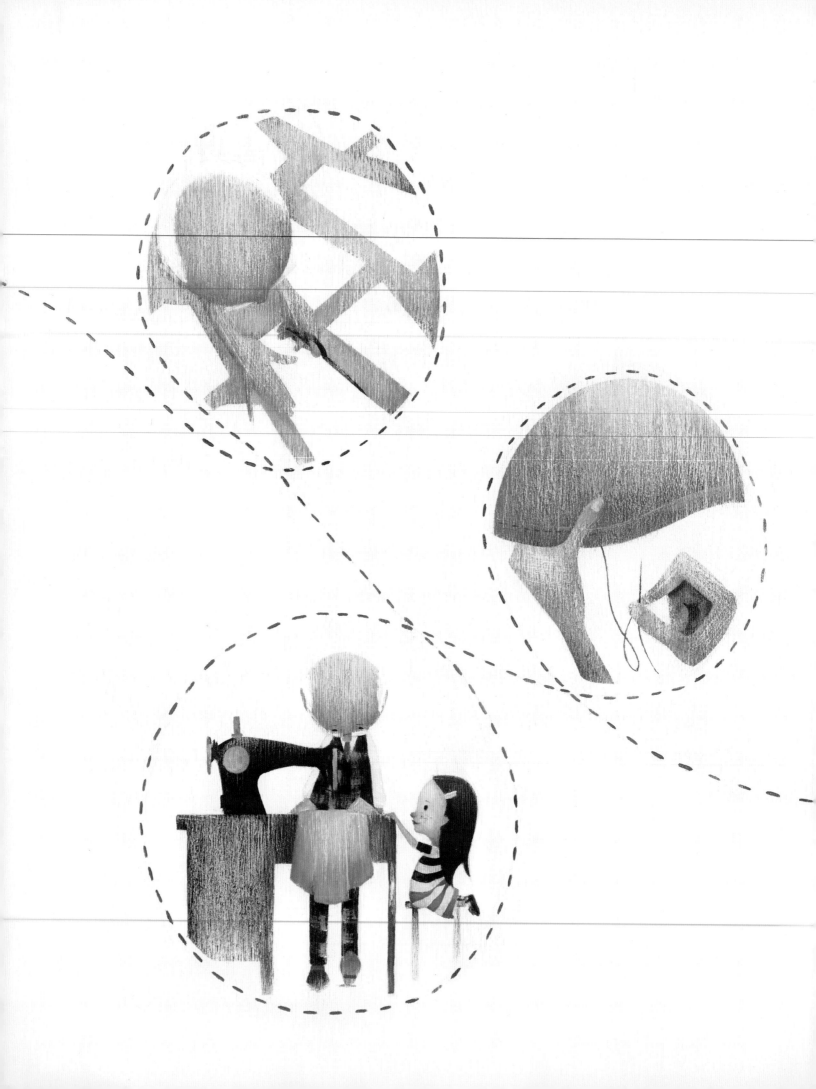

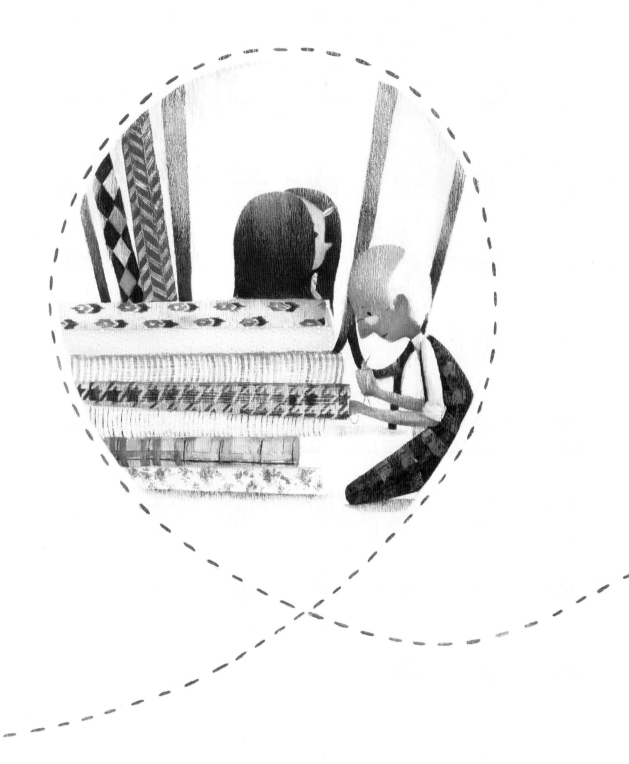

Then he cuts out the pieces of fabric, pins them together
and begins to sew. He works all afternoon.

When it's time for a fitting, Pepper stands patiently as
Mr. Taylor makes a few last alterations. The dress is finally ready!

"Your perfect pattern is paisley," Mr. Taylor says. "A very old pattern inspired by pinecones, the shoots of a date palm and the pods of cashew fruit. Paisley was created in Kashmir, India, where it was used for hand-woven shawls, and later it became popular in the town of Paisley, Scotland, where the pattern got its name."

Pepper hugs Mr. Taylor. "Thank you, Mr. Taylor! It IS perfect," she says. "I can't wait to wear it!"

Pepper puts on her new dress for her special day.
She arrives at her grandma's house for an afternoon
of tea and croquet in the garden.

"Happy birthday, Grandma! I love your
herringbone dress," she says.

Pepper and her grandma sip tea, eat scones
and whack balls through hoops under the
summer sun, each in her own perfect pattern.